Ours to Love

The Brotherhood Series:
Book 3

Nia JoLove

Table of Content

Chapter 1: Jasmine

It was Saturday morning. Jasmine looked around at the salon filled with people and smiled. The smooth sounds of India Arie's song, "I Am Not My Hair" played in the background. All 10 chairs had clients in the different processes of getting their hair or nails done. The white and black decor gave the salon a modern feel. The small water feature at the front entrance provided a spa-like atmosphere. Murals of women with afros, twists, and locs hairstyles were displayed on many of the walls.

"Jasmine, what are you smiling about?" asked Imani, the hairstylist who was also considered a friend.

"I am just happy about how everything is going," stated Jasmine.

"Nah," said Imani, "you are just happy because you are getting married in two weeks." She laughed at that bit of information. "You're gettin' married, you're havin' babies," sung Imani as she returned to her client.

Jasmine continued to look around at the salon. She had built Salon New Vogue into one of the hottest salons in the Atlanta area. She catered to celebrity clients as well as the everyday working woman. In the beginning, she worked hard to get new clients and to find the best stylist. She used social media marketing to get the word out about the business. Now, most of her day was spent managing staff and making sure the operation of the business went smoothly.

Sometimes, she would take a client when the hairstylists were busy.

"Angela, I can see you in the next chair," Jasmine said to the younger woman who was interested in trying the knotless braid hairstyle. Jasmine adjusted the black cape around her client's neck. "Let's get you washed," said Jasmine as she took Angela to the wash area to shampoo and condition her hair before starting the braids.

Jasmine thought about her past as she washed the client's hair. She had come a long way from being raised by her grandmother after her parents died in a car accident. Just to think of it brought so much pain. "Is the water okay?" asked Jasmine.

"Yes, it's nice," said Angela.

"Tell me if it gets too hot," Jasmine questioned.

"You know I will," said Angela laughingly.

Continuing in thought, Jasmine remembered everything about the night her parents died. It was a nice day that became dark and stormy. They had asked Jasmine to watch Denise because she was the older sister. They wanted a date night. Jasmine was 15 and Denise was 10. This was a weekly occurrence and was a good way for Jasmine to make some extra money. Plus, they would always come back and never leave her and her sister for too long.

But that night, something wasn't right. Her parents slid off the road and hit a tree; they both died on impact. It was getting late and Jasmine heard a knock on the door. She would never open it but notice through the window that it was their grandmother. She walked in and gathered the girls together. She told them that their parents had died in a car accident.

Jasmine remembered both her and Denise crying hard and for so long. She remembered hugging her sister and trying to be strong, but she was only a teenager herself and didn't know how to deal with the emotions and feelings of death.

She believed that they would come back to them no matter what, but to her, they had broken their promises. Now, she and Denise were left alone. Their grandmother took custody of them and raised them. She gave them what they needed such as food, clothes, and shelter, but their grandmother was firm and was not as loving as she could have been. To come from a home that was filled with love to one that was lacking was a turnaround. This, in time, shaped Jasmine.

It was around 4:30 p.m. Jasmine and her staff were at a closing meeting. "Team, you did a wonderful job today!" said Jasmine. "Keep up the good work. Don't forget to continue your training on styling as well as maintaining natural hair. The more you know the more you can charge for your services." The staff cheered with excitement. "Have a great weekend," said Jasmine as each stylist filed out of the salon one by one.

Jasmine got in her black Mercedes Benz and drove off with her music blasting. She was off for the weekend, and it was time to relax. As she sang along to Lizzo's song, "Good as Hell," her phone rang, the car's Bluetooth displayed her sister's name, Denise.

"Hey Lady, what ya got going on?"

"Oh, just about to spend the weekend with Todd. I got my hair right with these new bundles and we're about to relax."

"You and your fiancé are having too much fun," said Denise with a hint of mischief in her voice.

"But anyways . . ." Jasmine said.

"I am so happy for you," Denise stated. "You and Todd are going to have a good wedding and a great marriage; Mom and Dad would be so proud of you." "Do you ever think of them?" asked Denise as she looked down at the phone awaiting her big sister's reply.

Jasmine answered, "Yes, most days I do—especially when there are big life changes like this wedding." You could hear the sorrow in her voice.

"I do too," said Denise.

"But it does get easier," said Jasmine as she tried to comfort her little sister.

"Jasmine, thanks for looking out for me when we were younger. You've always had my back," said Denise. Jasmine became very protective of Denise after their parents died. Whenever someone tried to pick on Denise, Jasmine would come to the school or wherever to take up for her.

"How is your acting career going?" asked Jasmine, trying to change the topic and get Denise to talk about something other than the past.

"Oh, it's great! We're almost finished wrapping up a movie at Tyler Perry Studios.

It's been nice having you here in Georgia. I'm going to miss you when you leave this week," Jasmine mentioned.

"Yes, it's great having my big Sis to hang with," said Denise.

Jasmine looked in the rearview mirror and noticed a black Impala behind her for three blocks. "Denise, I think I'm being followed," said Jasmine as she passed a block to stop at a light.

"What the hell?" stated Denise. "Why would you be followed?"

"I don't know," said Jasmine. Then the Impala noticed that Jasmine had slowed and turned the corner. Girl, maybe it was nothing; they just turned."

"Oh," said Denise, "you know they are taking women these days; you have to be careful."

"You're right, Denise."

"Bye Jasmine; stay safe," said Denise.

"Bye."

Jasmine made it home a few minutes later feeling a little eerie about the black Impala, but she was home now and had nothing to worry about.

Chapter 2: Todd

Jasmine walked into the home that she shared with Todd. Todd is a music producer, she met while doing a celebrity client's hair. She didn't mix business with pleasure, but he was different. Todd wasn't her normal type. He was tall with pale skin and dark brown, tapered hair. He came into the salon to see about getting his client's hair done for a music video, and Jasmine offered to cut his hair as well. They talked and hit it off. They had been dating for about a year when he proposed. Jasmine loved Todd, and the sex was great, but sometimes, she felt like something was missing. She agreed to marry him but wanted a long engagement. Now, two years later they are about to get married.

"Hey baby, I'm home," called Jasmine as she walked into the living room from the foyer. The house was immaculate with its four bedrooms and two bathrooms. It had vaulted ceilings in the living room and bay windows all around.

Todd rushed out of the office with two men in tow. "Hey, baby," said Todd. "These guys are just leaving."

"Who are they?" Jasmine asked curiously.

"Oh, just some people I'm working with." The men quickly left.

"Let's eat baby," said Todd. "I know you're hungry because you worked all day, and I know you didn't take a break. Todd gave Jasmine a sheepish smile. "Plus, I love taking care of my lady."

Todd entered the kitchen and took out the food that he had ordered. Jasmine loved how thoughtful Todd was, but she didn't like that he kept a ton of secrets. Todd kissed and hugged Jasmine. She didn't push or pry for more information. She would enjoy the food and time with Todd.

"How was your day, Todd?" asked Jasmine.

"It was good," Todd glanced at Jasmine questioningly. "What's on your mind, baby?"

"Well, I was just thinking about our free pass weekend coming up," said Jasmine.

"Baby, I know you love me, and I love you, but I want you to enjoy yourself before we are married. "We both get to do whatever and whomever we choose for the weekend only," said Todd.

"How do you feel about me sleeping with another man?" asked Jasmine.

"Obviously, I won't like it," said Todd, as his face went red. "But I understand that this is something you think you need to do so we can move forward with our life and marriage."

"How do you feel about me possibly sleeping with another woman?" asked Todd.

"I don't want to know about it," said Jasmine.

"Baby, I want you to live out all your desires and realize that I am not taking your freedom. I can't wait to marry you," said Todd.

Jasmine loved Todd for doing the free pass weekend. They could have sex with anyone they wanted and do anything they wanted but only this one time. Jasmine had fantasized about being with multiple partners. She wondered how it would feel to be intimate with two or three people at once. Having their hands and mouths ravishing her body sent shimmers through her skin straight to her pussy.

It wasn't something that Todd was into because he had experienced it before. Todd loved Jasmine. He wanted to make all of Jasmine's fantasies and dreams come true even if it meant sharing her with others for a weekend.

They both knew that their love was stronger than some fantasy. Recently, Jasmine began to think about it more and more. Also, because her friend Keira had married three men that loved and adored her. Kiera told her that being with all three at the same time was a mind-blowing experience.

Todd stood up and pulled Jasmine closer by the hand. "You are mine for tonight," he said as he smiled at Jasmine with a look of desire in his eyes. He got even closer to her and put his hands around her small waist. She was wearing a fitted blue dress. "Baby, you feel so good," he moaned in a sexy voice. Todd wanted to prove his love for Jasmine the only way he knew how.

Todd led Jasmine by the hand to the bathroom. He turned on the shower, making sure the temperature wasn't too hot. "Jaz, let me take care of you tonight." He kneeled in front of her. Next, he slid her lacy black panties down, letting them fall to the floor. He raised the dress to show her toned caramel legs. He pushed the dress even higher to reveal her shaved mound. He bent his head kissing first at the apex of her leg. Jasmine moaned Todd's name in anticipation.

"I want you so bad, Jasmine," said Todd in between licks. Then, he licked her bud slowly at first. Jasmine grabbed Todd's hair, forcing him closer. Then, Todd sucked her clit in his mouth. Jasmine released a moan at the contact.

"Todd, this feels so good; yes, so good, baby."

Next, Todd pressed one finger inside Jasmine's wet pussy.

"You want more, baby?" Todd asked Jasmine.

"Yes, I want more," said Jasmine.

Todd slid a second finger into Jasmine's stretching her tight cunt. Then, he scissored his fingers. Todd began sucking Jasmine's clit again while his fingers worked her pussy. Jasmine moaned louder and louder. She rocked on Todd's mouth and fingers.

"I am close, baby," she yelled.

Todd increased the tempo of his fingers and sucked harder on the bud. Next, he caressed her breast first the left then the right rotating between them. The steam from the running shower filled the air. All the sensations had Jasmine reeling. She let off like a rocket, squirting cum deep into Todd's throat. She rode his mouth as the cum released from her body. Todd looked up at Jasmine with love in his eyes. She rubbed his face.

"Let's take a shower." She knew that there was more to come.

Todd took off his clothes. They both stepped into the shower with the rainfall showerhead. Todd's dick was so hard. He needed to take Jasmine fast. "Face the wall, Jasmine," Todd commanded. "I need you like this now." Jasmine faced the wall.

She felt Todd kiss her neck and shoulders, but she also felt him slide his hard cock swiftly into her. She was still wet from the foreplay, and the water added even more slickness. First, his rhythm was slow. He whispered sweet words as he took her from behind. But as he grew even harder he began to pound faster and faster. He moaned louder and louder. "Jasmine, see what you do to me?" He stroked Jasmine's clit while pounding. He kissed her neck. She moaned his name and held on to the shower bar.

"Todd. Todd."

He had done so much in his past and now. His music business was going under which forced him to get creative with making money. He didn't want to lose his business or Jasmine. The music industry had changed. Before the Digital Age, all you needed was a good artist and connections in the business. Now, you need a good artist, connections in the business, plus marketing and branding. With YouTube and Facebook, artists were being signed based on the followers they already had built up. With new social media sites like TikTok, it was hard trying to keep up with the latest technology or marketing. Plus, he couldn't tell Jasmine about the business going under. *But If I could get one last score, Jasmine and I would be set for life,* thought Todd. Hearing Jasmine's moans growing louder brought Todd back from thinking too much to focus on what he and Jasmine were doing now. Todd could feel Jasmine's pussy tighten and sucked the cum out of him. He shook as he released the last drop of cum inside of Jasmine.

"I love you Jaz," said Todd as he leaned his head against Jasmine.

"I love you too, Todd." They showered and went to bed to bask in the afterglow of their lovemaking.

The next morning, Todd helped Jasmine pack for her trip. He slipped a little something extra into her suitcase. The free pass weekend starts tomorrow. Jasmine would drive to Florida, where she had rented a hotel room. She had an idea of who she would use her free pass with but didn't want anyone to know. She thought about three guys she went to college with and hoped she could meet with them.

"Jaz, be careful while driving," Todd said. "I already filled your tank with gas, so you won't have to stop for anything."

"I love the way you take care of me, Todd," said Jasmine. "I'm going to miss you so much." Closing the distance between them, Jasmine kissed Todd. It started slowly but deepened to give Todd something to remember her by.

"Todd, come on, I have to leave. I don't want to drive while it's dark."

Todd walked Jasmine to the car.

"Take care babe, and be safe."

Chapter 3: Road Trip

Jasmine started on her three-hour road trip to Florida. During the trip, she decided to call Kiera. "Keke what are you up to?" said Jasmine. "Do you have a minute to talk?"

"Yes, I was just feeding baby Ken." Keira's new baby could be heard in the background.

"Let me give Ken to one of his fathers." Returning to the phone, she asked, "What's going on Jasmine? How are you and Todd?"

"Everything is great, KeKe. Todd and I are doing fine, but this weekend is the free pass weekend."

Both ladies screamed with excitement.

"I can't believe that Todd let you do this with the wedding so close."

"Todd didn't let me do this, KeKe. I control my body, and no man is going to tell me what to do," said Jasmine in a sarcastic voice. Both women laughed again. "It's happening KeKe, but I have some doubts.

What if Todd can't take what I am doing? What if this free pass weekend messes up what we have?"

"No worries, Jasmine. Todd loves you," Kiera reaffirmed. "You and Todd have been through so much together. "Plus, he knew you were a freak when he met you."

"And you know that's right," said Jasmine.

"You guys will be just fine," Kiera said.

"Thanks, Kiera."

"Is Todd still being secretive?" asked Kiera.

"Yes, I just feel like he has something going on that I don't know about. I feel like he has a wall up that keeps us from going deeper in this relationship." Jasmine looked out the front window in the distance and rubbed her hand over her curly sew-in.

"You have to talk to him, Jasmine, tell him how you feel," said Kiera.

"Yes, I have to talk to him. I want to marry Todd, but I'm not sure about all the secrets."

"Don't worry about this now Jaz," Kiera said. "Enjoy your weekend. When you come back, you and Todd can figure it out together."

"Okay, Keke, enough about me. Tell me about those fine men of yours," Jasmine said.

"Oh, they're doing great," Kiera exclaimed. "Jackson just returned from a trip with some of his buddies in his unit. Eric is working on some security software, and Jamal is helping out in the community."

"Keke, you know that I am *not* talking about work and stuff. Tell me the goodies. Are they still making you scream in bed?" asked Jasmine.

"Of course, and more!" said Kiera. "They always manage to push me further sexually, but it's more than that. The connection to all the men is unbelievable. In the beginning, I didn't know how it all would work, but now, I wouldn't have it any other way. Each man thrills me physically, mentally, and sexually."

"That's exactly what I need, Keke, but I don't have it now with Todd," Jasmine said sadly. "Hopefully that will change."

"It will, Jaz, don't worry. Enjoy this weekend. You are so brave to go after what you want."

"Thanks, Keke, and thanks for the advice."

"Don't forget to check-in and let me know how things are going," said Kiera.

"You know I will," said Jasmine. Each friend said bye and hung up the phone. Jasmine continued on her way to Florida. She didn't know what it had in store for her, but she was open to new possibilities and opportunities. She would live life to the fullest and worry about Todd later.

Chapter 4: The Men

The clanking of metal hitting metal could be heard all around JAM CrossFit gym. As the smell of sweat wafted through the air, people lifted weights, pulled ropes, and flipped tires.

Jackson added to the clanking sound by picking up the 190-pound weight, lifting it 10 times as his homeboy spotted him.

Mike lifted the barbell in sets of five reps as he listened to his brothers talk. "Yo man, business has been really good," said Jackson. A former professional football player, started JAM CrossFit after a back injury ended his football career.

"Yes," laughed Andre. "Who knew that these dingy gyms would turn a profit so fast?"

"What dingy gyms are you talking about?" asked Mike. "We built each gym from the ground up with industry quality equipment and the best people we could find."

They both laughed because Jackson and Mike knew Andre was playing around.

Andre was the finance guy for the gyms. In the past, he started and closed many companies, but nothing worked until he, Jackson, and Mike started JAM CrossFit gym.

Jackson, Andre, and Mike attended college together back in the day. While hanging out, they made a pack to finish school together. During this time, they got close. It was three young men from the hood trying to do something better for themselves. But college was a challenge.

They were the first to go in their family. They all had freedom, so at first, they partied and sexed so many women. Most times money was tight. Plus, they felt like they weren't prepared for college life. They struggled academically and financially until they came together— each helping one another. Andre would help with math or any course. Mike had a job, so he would help pay for books. Somehow, Jackson would get food even if it was just ramen noodles. They shared everything, and soon, they started sharing women. It was something to see their homeboy getting his dick sucked while they pounded the same girl from the back.

This strengthened their bond and enabled them to finish college. After college, Jackson was drafted by the Florida Bucks to play football. Andre got a degree in business and finance and started a few businesses. Mike went to medical school and became a physical therapist.

Everything was going great until it wasn't. Jackson played for the Bucks for five years until a back injury cost him everything. He lost his job and house, and the woman he was dating eventually left.

Andre saw some success with his business until the economy crashed. He had invested everything in businesses, but one by one, they began to fail. He lost his house, and his wife left due to the stress from finances.

Mike was a physical therapist who had celebrity clients because of his connection with Andre. He would travel around, offering his services whenever an athlete was injured. He was able to help them heal quicker with his techniques and methods. But his travels kept him away from his home and his wife. Eventually, she left him for another man because he wasn't there.

Each man was broken and had a lot of baggage. They pooled what money they had left to buy a large house in Florida that they shared. Jackson came up with the idea to start the JAM CrossFit gym, so he asked Andre to help him run it and Mike to add physical therapy as a service. The business has been booming since.

Yet one thing was missing: a woman who they could satisfy and love. They tried to have their own woman, but it always failed because the business or job kept them away for long hours. With three men, there would always be someone to take care of their woman.

"Hey bros, how about we go to Jazzy's tomorrow to celebrate the opening of our new JAM CrossFit gym?" asked Jackson. "This would make the 10th location that we own. We need to start celebrating this success."

"You're right! Plus, this will give us a chance to meet with the ladies," Andre said as he rubbed his face.

Mike agreed: "Yes, I could relax to some smooth jazz music and soul food. He put the barbell back on the rack. "Bet," said Jackson as they made plans to go to Jazzy's the next day.

Chapter 5: The Club

The smooth sound of the saxophone could be heard outside of Jazzy's Club. Cars parked along the street meant that the house was packed tonight.

Jackson, Andre, and Mike walked into the club each dressed in suites ranging in colors from black to gray. "You'll know we look good," said Andre as he ran his hand over his short, twisted hair that he was growing into locs. Andre was six feet tall, lean-built with dark, mocha-kissed skin.

"Yes, we do look alright," said Jackson as he rubbed his beard. It was something he did often when he was confident or feeling himself. Jackson was six feet four inches of hotness. He was a big guy but light on his feet. His chest was wide and held his shoulders like a linebacker would hold the ball. But Jackson was down to earth and would give you the shirt off his back.

"But I look the best," teased Mike. His gray Armani suit with a pink shirt underneath was cut just right.

Mike was the shortest of the group at 5'11" but held his own with the brothers.

"Come on guys, let's get some drinks," said Jackson as he led his team to the bar. They selected their drinks and sat at a table near the back. Most people sipped on drinks while moving their heads to the beat. An older couple swayed back and forth on the dance floor as they gazed into each other's eyes. The serene sounds of the saxophone floated through the air, while the bass guitar set the pace for the Coltrane song "Blue Train" that was playing.

In the far corner stood a group of newly minted girls excited about being allowed in the club for the first time. As the night went by, the crowd grew and the music went from jazz to more pop and hip hop. The hood crews started arriving.

Chapter 6: We Meet Again

Jasmine entered the club, arriving ahead of her friend, and went to the bar to order her signature drink piña colada. Checking her phone for the third time, she called her friend Samantha. "Hey Sam, I thought you would be here by now," said Jasmine after Sam picked up.

Cough, Cough, "I just can't shake this cold. I thought it would be gone by tonight, but it's only gotten worse, said Sam"

"Oh, no, said Jasmine. "I hope you feel better. Get some rest, and I'll call you in the morning." Jasmine hung up the phone.

What should I do, she thought? *I got dressed in the outfit and did my hair, and I don't want to waste it.* She looked around the bar and thought she saw three familiar faces, but she had been drinking, so she shook her head and continued drinking and listening to the music.

Jackson felt his skin tingle. He looked around.

"Hey, is that Jasmine from college at the bar?"

Andre and Mike looked at the bar and spotted Jasmine. "Whoa. Yeah, that's her," they both said at the same time.

"Let's go talk to her," said Jackson. All three of the men went to speak with Jasmine.

"Jasmine, is that you?" said Jackson. "What are you doing in Florida?" A smile came over Jasmine's face.

"Jackson! Yes, it's me! I am here in Florida for a week on vacation." She didn't want them to know about the free pass week. One by one, she gave them hugs. She wanted the hugs to linger because something felt right and familiar, but she let them go.

"Come sit with us at our table so we can catch up," said Andre as he led Jasmine to the table by her hand. The connection between them all was surreal. It had been years since she had seen them when they all attended college together. They all flirted with her, but it never went anywhere. She didn't know if they liked her sexually or just thought of her as a sister. Now, the way her body reacted to them, she hoped it would be more.

"Jasmine, what have you been up to?" asked Jackson over the music thumping in the background. He moved a little closer so she could hear him; Mike and Andre move closer as well.

"Things have been going well," said Jasmine. "I finished school with a bachelor's degree in business. For a while, I managed different businesses until I started a hair salon in Georgia. It's doing quite well. How about you?" asked Jasmine as she looked into his dark brown eyes.

It made Jackson rub his beard. "I played football for the Bucks until I was injured. Now Andre, Mike, and I own a few JAM CrossFit gyms,"

"Oh, I am glad you're doing well," said Jasmine. I followed your career a little after college and was impressed, to say the least."

"Thank you, Jackson said as he blushed. He tried to hide it as best as he could.

"How about you, Andre? What's your story?" asked Jasmine.

"I started a few businesses, and a few failed, but now I am part owner-manager of JAM CrossFit gyms, and I love it. I get to be with my homeboys, and the company is making a profit. "

Lastly, Mike spoke: "Well, for me, I am a physical therapist for JAM CrossFit gyms. It's amazing to be able to help people heal and get healthy." Mike was a people person. He was compassionate and had the heart to help.

"Okay, guys, enough about work. We are here to relax," said Jasmine as she moved her arms to the music. They wanted to ask Jasmine if she was dating or married, but she beat them to it.

"Hey, guys are you dating anyone?" Jasmine asked.

"We haven't found the right one," Andre said as he looked into her brown eyes.

"What about Jackson and Mike?" asked Jasmine.

"No," they both replied as they shook their heads.

"What about you Jasmine?" asked Jackson?

"I . . . I . . . It's complicated," said Jasmine. Jasmine knew she should tell the guys up-front that she was about to be married but thought it would mess up what would be an interesting night, so she left it as complicated. Looking around at the men, Jasmine asked, "Does anyone want to dance?"

The music had changed, and now, a slow song was playing. Jackson linked hands with Jasmine and led her to the dance floor, while Andre and Mike looked on. They squeeze through people into an open space near the front. Jackson placed Jasmine's hands around his neck and gently placed his hands around her waist. She closed her eyes and inhaled. Damn, he smelled good. "You know Jasmine, I had feelings for you back in the day," he whispered in her ear. Jasmine, letting down her guard a little, let her head relax on Jackson's broad shoulders.

"We all had feelings for you," said Jackson as he held her closer so she could feel the girth of his shaft.

"Oh," said Jasmine as she moved even closer. "I liked you all, too, but I heard about how you guys shared women back in the days. What was that about?"

"Yes, but it's not like that," Jackson said as he continued explaining. "In college, things were rough. We weren't doing well financially or academically. We bonded together to finish college. We did everything together and that eventually led to us sharing women. Now, I just want the best for my homeboys and to see them happy. We don't mind sharing one woman who we can satisfy and love. We would have a family together. There would be no jealousy or strife. Just a few men taking care of their lady and home." Jasmine looked into Jackson's eyes and saw sheer honesty—something she didn't have with Todd. She wanted to be that for the guys, but she didn't know. After the song finished, they returned to the table.

"Can I have the next dance?" asked Andre.

"Of course," said Jasmine.

Andre gently pulled Jasmine by the waist and led her to another area of the dance floor but not before giving her a peck at the nape. Andre then spun Jasmine around to face him.

"This song has a good beat," said Jasmine which allowed Andre to show off his moves. He swung his hips and thrust a little in the air. "Whoa, you got some moves," said Jasmine as she looked on with her mouth open.

"Thanks, Jasmine," he said as he moved closer and closer. He caressed her arm.

"You know I had feelings for you, and I still do," said Andre. "Back in the day, I liked the way you were always there for us when we needed you. Jasmine, I thought about you a lot."

Time seemed to stand still for Jasmine. She loved the way Andre was honest and shared his feelings with her.

"Jasmine, I have been hurt in the past, and now, I am looking for love."

Jasmine looked at the seriousness in Andre's eyes. She stood on her tiptoes and lightly kissed him on the lips. As she became familiar with his lips, she took the kiss deeper. Feeling the urge, Andre took control. His hands moved up and down Jasmine's back. He probed Jasmine's mouth. He could taste the piña colada on her lips. Not wanting to embarrass himself or Jasmine anymore, Andre pulled away and put his head on Jasmine's head.

"I see there is definitely still a connection. I don't know what it is about you, Jasmine. When I am with you, I feel different."

"Umm . . ."

Jasmine and Andre turned to see Mike standing next to them.

"Do you mind if I cut in, brother?" asked Mike. "I want to dance with Jasmine."

"Sure thing, said Andre as he gave Jasmine a quick kiss on the lips before leaving the dance floor. Mike and Jasmine swayed to the seductive sounds of the music.

"Jasmine, I had a crush on you back in the day," said Mike in his baritone voice. "It's because you have always shown compassion to those in need. I remember back in college when you worked with the Salvation Army going door to door to feed the elderly." Jasmine coyly smiled. "I remember you going too and offering medical services to those in need. I didn't realize that you had noticed me," said Mike. "Oh, I did," said Jasmine. "What's not to notice? Tall, dimples, and smart." Mike smiled and held Jasmine closer.

After the song, they went back to their table. Jasmine realized that being with each guy was different but not in a bad way. She wanted to explore what they had to offer.

Chapter 7: Shots Fired

Pop, Pop, Pop.

Shots were fired throughout the club. The music stopped playing, and everyone became eerily quiet. The masked gunman stood on the stage with his crew. "Jasmine Harris, we know you're in the building. Give us our fucking stuff. If not, we will start shooting up the place. Todd told us you have it!" The crowd went wild. People started screaming and running for the exit. Those who were too drunk to run got stampeded in the aftermath. Jasmine nearly fainted hearing her name from the masked man and hearing Todd's name. *What the fuck?!* Was all she could think. *"What the fuck?*

Let's get the hell out of here!" commanded Jackson as he grabbed Jasmine by the arm. Mike and Andre followed closely behind. Making sure to protect Jasmine, they covered her with their bodies. They pushed through the people until they were outside of the club.

"Jasmine, you have to go with us," said Jackson as he led her and his boys to the car. They drove for 20 minutes until they reached a vacant parking garage.

Jasmine stood before the men with a look of dismay on her face.

"Tell us what the hell is going on!" yelled Jackson as he paced back and forth.

"Hold on just a damn minute," said Mike. "Jasmine is just as upset as we are about the situation. Let's hear her out."

Visibly shaken Jasmine spoke: "I don't know what the hell is going on. The only thing I know is that I was here on a sort of vacation before I got married."

"What the hell, Jasmine! You're about to get married?"

"It's not like that," said Jasmine. "It's complicated. We were taking a break, and now all this has happened. I don't know what the masked men want or who the hell they are. I am just scared and don't know what to do."

"Is Todd your fiancé?" asked Andre. "That's the name that the masked men said."

"Yes, but we are on a break this week. We are supposed to be able to do what we want and explore," Jasmine said as she looked down at the pavement. "But I don't know who the masked men are or what they want." Before Jasmine could explain more, her phone rang. She dug it out of her Louis Vuitton bag, and seeing Todd's name on the caller ID, she answered the phone.

"Todd, what the hell is going on?"

"Shut the hell up! This is not Todd. We have Todd and his phone. We just beat the shit out of him and will do the same to you if you don't give us the fucking shit."

Jasmine started crying and shaking.

"Listen real close," said the caller. Todd said he put the stuff in your suitcase." Jasmine could hear the faint sounds of Todd groaning in the background. He sounded like he was in pain. "Get your fucking suitcase and meet us, or we will kill him and you. Don't call the cops, or it will all be over. Do you get it?!" yelled the caller.

"Y . . . yes," said Jasmine.

"Todd knew the consequences of not giving us our stuff."

"What stuff are you talking about? What did he put in my suitcase?" asked Jasmine.

"Just get the damn stuff and meet us in two days." The caller hung up.

Jasmine screamed then threw the phone back into her purse. "Shit! Shit! Shit!" Her mind started racing trying to figure out how to help Todd. "They kidnapped Todd and now want me to bring some stuff that he put in my suitcase, or they will kill him and me!"

"Those assholes!" yelled Andre.

"Okay, let's all calm down," said Jackson. "Our priority is to protect Jasmine."

"Let's take her to our house so we can develop a plan. We can use the element of surprise because they don't know we are protecting her," Mike suggested. They got into the car and drove to their home, while Jasmine tried to piece together what was going on in her head. Mike and Andre sat in the back seat holding her. They told her that things would be alright. She could count on them to protect her. "Jasmine, we will keep you safe."

Chapter 8: At the House

The car ride to the guys' house took about 30 minutes —just enough time to settle down from the events that occurred. "Jasmine, We are going to protect you," said Jackson.

"There's no need to worry," Andre agreed. "We have everything you need from clothes to a big fancy pool," joked Andre to lighten the mood.

"I don't want to be a bother to you. I know you all have a lot going on," said Jasmine in a soft voice.

This unraveled Jackson because he had never heard Jasmine's voice sound so small and fragile. She was always full of life even during tough times.

"Jasmine, it's no problem; you are our priority now." All the guys shook their heads in agreement.

Mike held Jasmine's hand. Jasmine turned her face to him and gave a half-smile. Mike's groin began to throb. He shouldn't feel this way about Jasmine with everything that was going on. How could she elicit a reaction from him like this? She was smart and very sexy. She had feelings for him and all the guys. He would have to explore the feelings as he reacquainted himself with her.

Mike and Andre helped Jasmine exit the car at a beautiful Mediterranean-style home with an Italian roof. It was on about seven acres of land with a gated entrance. The outside of the house was lit with a soft glow of lights.

Jasmine's mouth dropped when she saw the house. "This is an amazing house," Jasmine said. She wasn't used to the style because many of the homes in Georgia were plantation-style.

"Wait until you see the inside," said Jackson as he smiled and unlocked the door. Jasmine's face lit up when she saw the inside of the house.

"I can't believe you all live here!"

"It's spacious; we all have separate rooms and living areas," said Mike.

Jasmine and the men walked into the large living room overlooking a pool with the ocean as a backdrop. The furniture was modern with clean lines. The open concept kitchen and dining room made it easy to look through the house with one sweep.

Andre locked the door. It felt good to have a lady in the house even though she was there under extenuating circumstances. He set the code for the alarm to ensure they were safe.

"Jasmine, let Mike show you to your room while we give you a chance to relax. Fellas, let's meet in the dining room to discuss the plans. Jasmine, when you are ready, please join us," said Jackson.

Mike showed Jasmine to her room upstairs. It was on the second story of the house where all the bedrooms were located.

"Jasmine, this is your room," said Mike. "Everything you need is here. There are extra clothes that may fit you in the closet. In the bathroom, there are toiletry items and fresh towels." Jasmine turned and gave Mike a big hug.

"Thank you so much for everything that you and the guys are doing for me. I appreciate it."

Mike released Jasmine from the hug, even though he didn't want to. "If you need anything else, we are downstairs and will be happy to get it for you."

With that, Mike left Jasmine in the room. Jasmine looked around at the finely decorated room. There was a king-size poster bed in the middle of the room. Jasmine walked to the plush-looking bed and sat down. *What am I even doing here?* Jasmine thought. *Maybe I should've gone to the police first. This has been one hell of a day.* Then Jasmine began to think about the guys. So far they had been understanding. They told her they would protect her, and she believed them. Plus, she had a connection with all of them. Every time she was around one of the men, her stomach would tighten.

Jasmine went to the closet to check for some clothes. There were T-shirts, jeans, and dresses that she could fit. There was also a new bathing suit that she would use to relax in the pool. After finding some pajamas, Jasmine went to take a shower. Jasmine didn't know where things were going. She didn't know what was going on with Todd, and she didn't know what staying with the guys would be like. But she hoped that they felt the connection for her, and they would explore. After the long, hot shower, Jasmine felt better. She felt more like herself. She went downstairs to discuss the plan with the guys.

As Jasmine walked down the stairs, she saw the guys sitting at the dining room table. Each man looked up at Jasmine as she descended the stairs.

Her almond skin glowed from the shea butter lotion. Her curly hair was pulled in a top bun. The two-piece nightgown showed her long shapely legs. The way the guys looked at her caused Jasmine to exhale softly. Her stomach tightened and sent tingles to her pussy.

"Jasmine, how do you feel?" Jackson asked.

"It's been a long day, but the shower and the clean clothes helped out. Thank you so much for what you've done."

"It's no problem," said Jackson.

"Would you like something to eat?" asked Andre.

"We picked up some fried rice and chicken from the Chinese restaurant around the corner," Mike said. Jasmine's stomach growled: "Yes, fried rice and chicken sounds good." Jasmine sat at the dining room table with the men.

"Let's get started," said Jackson. What we've found out while you were upstairs is that the club was shot up. No one was hurt, but the police don't have any leads." Jasmine looked into Jackson's eyes. Her face was downcast.

"I can't believe this is happening," Jasmine said. "This was supposed to be a fun weekend, but now, everything is messed up."

"Jasmine, don't worry, we will help you. It's good that they didn't see us slip out of the club. Also, they don't know what they are up against. They probably just think it's you, but we have resources and know this city," Jackson said as he tried to calm Jasmine's fears by rubbing her shoulders.

"Plus, the security system here is top-notch," added Andre.

Mike stood up. "Jasmine, did you want anything to drink?"

"Yeah, I'm going to need something strong tonight."

After dinner, the men and Jasmine came up with a plan to get the suitcase and exchange it for the safety of Todd.

Chapter 9: The Next Day

The next day, Jasmine woke feeling a little bit anxious but glad that she was safe with the men. She washed her face and grabbed some clothes from the closet before going downstairs.

Entering the kitchen, She noticed Andre and Mike fixing breakfast.

"Good morning, guys," said Jasmine.

"Good Morning, Jasmine!" they said in unison.

"Hopefully we didn't wake you, and you were able to get some sleep," said Mike.

"How did you sleep?" asked Andre.

Jasmine replied, "I slept well, considering everything that's going on."

"Come have some breakfast with us," Andre said. "Are eggs and bacon okay?"

"Yes, eggs and bacon are great," said Jasmine. "Where is Jackson?" asked Jasmine.

"He had to go to the office, but he should be back this afternoon," said Andre. "He wanted to ensure everything was running smoothly."

"So, what should we do while we wait for Jackson to return?"

"How about we go for a swim? asked Mike. "This will help us all relax," said Andre. Last night was so intense.

"And I have a bathing suit upstairs," said Jasmine as she went to change.

Mike and Andre were in the pool when Jasmine returned. Her bathing suit fit her amazingly. It was yellow with high cuts on both sides which accented her long legs. Her breasts were naturally large with only a triangle piece of fabric covering her nipples.

Mike's groin began to enlarge at the sight of her. "Come in," said Andre, "the water feels great." Andre swam toward Jasmine and helped her get into the pool. He put his arms around her waist.

She could feel how excited he was to see her.

"Jasmine, I know I am always joking and playing, but I am serious about exploring this connection we have."

Jasmine pressed closer to Andre's groin.

"I lost everything when the economy went bad. When you lose your family, too, that makes things worse." Andre held Jasmine closer. He wanted her to feel how sincere he was about his feelings.

"But now with my boys, things are almost in place. I am just missing a deeper connection and love."

Jasmine began to tremble in his arms.

"I lost my mom and dad when I was a teenager," said Jasmine. "I still think about them often."

"I'm sorry, Jasmine. That must be so tough," Andre said as he tightened his arms around Jasmine's waist. He wanted to take her pain and sorrows away.

He held her for what felt like hours but was only a few minutes.

She didn't quite understand how deep his feelings were for her, but she knew that she wanted to explore what he was offering. Andre kissed Jasmine lightly on the neck. "I like this," said Jasmine. "I don't know where it will lead, but I want to explore as well."

Jasmine leaned her head to the left so Andre could have better access. He rubbed his hand down the front of her bathing suit. Mike swam up next to them.

"Do you mind if I join?"

"No, I sure don't mind," said Andre. They wanted to make sure Jasmine was relaxed and pleased.

"Jasmine, do you mind if I join?" asked Mike. "Please do," said Jasmine. She didn't know how the day would turn out, but she thought it was about to be very good.

Mike stepped closer and kissed her on the lips while Andre kissed her on the neck from behind. Andre's hands rubbed her breast and nipples on top of the bathing suit.

Jasmine moaned in Mike's mouth. She felt warm, and her body tingled all over between the two men. She rubbed Andre's cock from behind and Mike's cock from the front.

The water reached up to their thighs. Caressing her through the bathing suit, Mike ached with desire. "Jasmine, do you want Mike to touch your pussy? I think he would like it very much." "Yes," said Jasmine as she arched toward Mike. Andre looked on as Mike pushed the yellow bikini bottoms to the side and inserted a finger inside of Jasmine's wet, tight pussy.

"She's so tight," Mike said to Andre. Jasmine moaned louder.

"Yes, yes," she whispered.

"How does it feel with Mike's finger inside of you? Do you want more?" asked Andre, holding her with one hand and squeezing her breast with the other. His cocked strained against his swimming trunks and her backside. He was so turned on by his friend finger fucking Jasmine. He wanted to bend her over the side of the pool and shove his cock inside of her again and again. But he also wanted to make it good for her, so he would wait until she was even more aroused.

Jasmine began to shake as her climax neared. She could feel it building up. She wanted to feel their cocks thrusting inside of her.

"Let Mike taste your pussy," said Andre. Mike went to his knees in the shallow waters of the pool. Andre spread Jasmine's legs further apart to let Mike in. Mike opened Jasmine's lips with his thumb and index fingers. He looked on in amazement.

"Her pussy is so pink," said Mike as he gazed at her.

Jasmine wanted to close her legs because she felt a little shy. She had never been looked at like this before. Mike bent his head to taste Jasmine. He lapped at her clit. At the contact, Jasmine whimpered.

"Dre, she tastes so damn good," said Mike. Andre looked on and held Jasmine by the waist as Mike pressed his tongue inside Jasmine's wet passage. Jasmine moaned.

Andre enjoyed watching and hearing both his friend and Jasmine give and receive pleasure. Mike released Jasmine's bud from his mouth and looked up at Andre.

"Dre, I could use some help. Open Jasmine's folds while I eat her pussy real good."

"Hah, bet," Andre said. Andre slid his hands down the front until he reached the junction of Jasmine. He gently opened Jasmine's pussy lips as he held her from the back.

Mike sucked relentlessly on her nub and inserted one large finger, then two. He pumped her with his digits.

Jasmine began to shake. I am about to cum she cried. She tried to hold on, but with two men working her pussy, it was hard.

Andre and Mike sucked, licked, and lavished kisses everywhere on Jasmine. The water from the pool rocked back and forth.

Jasmine grabbed Mike's head and held it to her as she thrust her hips. She could feel her orgasm about to explode. She pumped Andre's cock from behind. Mike pushed his fingers deeper and deeper inside of Jasmine's wanting cunt. Jasmine was pushed to the edge. She came so hard and much that it filled Mike's mouth and her legs felt weak.

The guys' cocks stood at attention through their trunks. "Jasmine, let's finish this out of the water," said Andre.

Andre carried Jasmine out of the water and placed her on Mike's lap in a lounge chair.

She could feel how much Mike wanted her, and it turned her on more. Mike removed her bikini top, and Andre removed her bottoms. Her pussy juices flowed down to her ass. Mike lifted Jasmine to remove his shorts. Andre stood in front of Jasmine and removed his shorts as well.

Mike loved the feel of Jasmine's wet pussy so close to his cock. If he inched over a little, he could pound her a lot.

Jasmine licked her lips at the sight of Andre's dick. She wanted to see what it tasted like. She pulled him forward by his waist. "Let me suck you," said Jasmine in her most seductive voice.

Andre's cock began to pulse with need.

"Yes, you can, but you have to take care of Mike's cock too by sitting on it." Mike lifted Jasmine by her waist and forged his cock to the hilt. He couldn't wait any longer.

Mike moaned. Jasmine's pussy tightened on Mike's cock.

She groaned, too.

"Jasmine, are you alright?" asked Mike.

"Yes, I just didn't realize how big your cock is."

Andre wrapped his hands in Jasmine's hair and guided her to his cock. She was still getting accustomed to the length and girth of Mike. But she became more comfortable as she rocked back and forth controlling the speed and tempo. She then took Andre's cockhead in her mouth. She gave special attention to the slit in the middle.

Andre could feel his orgasm building, and by the look on Mike's face, his was, too. The sight of Jasmine working her pink tongue over his cock had him about to bust.

"Damn, I won't last long like this Jasmine," Andre said.

"Neither will I," said Mike.

Jasmine's ass cheeks bounced up and down on Mike. This sent him reeling. He pounded faster from the bottom. His groin got even harder as he watched Jasmine suck his homeboy dick to the back of her throat. They all moved in unison. With one deep thrust, Mike erupted first. He growled and laid back with Jasmine still connected.

"Dre, give Jasmine more," said Mike as he pulled his cock from Jasmine's pussy. "I can tell she wants some more."

As he laid Jasmine back on top of him, he spread her legs wide with his legs, and he held her.

Andre stepped forward and kneeled in front of Jasmine and Mike. Her pussy was wet and filled with his friend's cum. He inched his cock into her as she laid on top of Mike. He moved slowly, looking into her eyes and taking in her expressions as he worked her pussy.

"Jasmine, you are so beautiful." She wanted to look away but was fascinated by his dark brown eyes and the way Andre was looking at her. Mike placed his hands between Jasmine and Andre to rub her nipples. He wanted to keep Jasmine on edge for his friend.

Andre kissed Jasmine hard and deep as he continued to stroke her passage.

"Jasmine, take all of me," said Andre. His long, hard strokes caused her to move up and down on Mike.

"I'm about to cum," said Jasmine.

Mike used his hands to spread Jasmine's legs even further apart.

"Dre, she's almost there," said Mike. "I can feel her shaking." Mike placed one hand in between Andre and Jasmine to stroke her clit.

"Cum for us, Jasmine," said Mike. Andre pumped faster and deeper. She closed her eyes because she couldn't take it anymore and released a yell.

"Fuck! Fuck! Fuck!" Jasmine came apart in Mike's arm with Andre's cock. As she was cumming, Andre groaned and erupted. Hot liquid spewed from Jasmine's overfilled cunt.

Andre collapsed on top of Jasmine and Mike. Jasmine was sandwiched between two men. She felt protected, safe, and satisfied.

***

Jasmine woke up to the phone ringing. It was the evening. The guys must have helped her to her room to take an afternoon nap after going at it for most of the morning. She grabbed it after she saw Samantha's name on the caller ID. *Oh shit, what time is it? She's probably worried*, thought Jasmine.

"Hey Sam, what's going on?"

"What's going on with you? I have been trying to call you for three hours! I was so worried about you. I heard there was a shooting at Jazzy, and I couldn't reach you," said Samantha in a teary voice.

"Sorry, Sam. I'm okay," reassured Jasmine. "There was a shooting at the club and some people are looking for me."

"What? " asked Samantha.

"They think I have something of theirs, and they have kidnapped Todd."

"You've got to call the police!" yelled Samantha.

"We can't!" shouted Jasmine. "They said they will kill me and Todd if we do!"

"Jasmine, you are alone, and I'm trying to help."

"I know you are trying to help Sam, but I'm actually not alone. I'm staying with three guys from college. They have been helping so far."

"Jasmine, do you trust them?"

Jasmine replied, "Yes, I do trust them. I have known them for a while."

"I just want you to be safe, Jasmine. What about Todd?"

"I'm not sure what he has to do with any of this, but I'm going to find out."

"Jasmine, you are like a sister to me so please be safe."

"Thanks, Sam. I have to take care of things. I really appreciate your concern."

"If I can do anything to help, please call me, Jasmine."

"I will, Sam," Jasmine said as she hung up. Jasmine got up to find the guys. She had to get her suitcase and help Todd.

Chapter 10: Jackson

Jasmine passed by Andre's and Mike's empty bedroom before going downstairs to the kitchen. In the kitchen, she came upon Jackson with his broad masculine back toward her.

"Hey, sleepyhead" said Jackson as she entered the kitchen.

"How did you know it was me?" asked Jasmine.

"I heard your footsteps upstairs. Plus, Andre and Mike went to the gym. I can also feel your energy. It's like a pull."

Jackson turned around and looked at Jasmine in her eyes. There was an attraction like Jackson had never felt before. He saw it in her eyes as well. He wondered if it could be more. Jackson smiled and rubbed his beard.

"Jasmine, you have to stop doing that to me."

"What am I doing?"

"You know, staring like you want something."

"Jackson, I have no idea what you are talking about," laughed Jasmine.

"Hey, would you like some dinner?" Jackson asked. "I know that we have to get the bag and save your fiancé, but this will give us a chance to talk."

Jasmine nodded. "Yes, dinner sounds nice."

Jasmine looked over the dinner that Jackson had prepared.

"Whoa, I didn't know that you can cook like this."

There were collard greens, chicken, cornbread, and peach cobbler.

***

"Jackson, everything smelled and tasted delicious," said Jasmine.

"Thank you, Jasmine. I learned to cook after my injury. I didn't have anyone for a while, and I got tired of frozen dinners and takeout."

"It must have been lonely," Jasmine stated.

"Yes, for a really long time. I was in a bad place." Jackson looked down at his food. Jasmine could see the hurt in his eyes. "That's when Mike and Andre came into my life again. True brothers: They are fam," said Jackson.

"Mike, the physical therapist nursed my body back to health. He helped motivate me to start walking and exercising. While Andre with his happy ass and jokes brought back my love of life. I would do anything for them, and they would do the same for me. Even though they were going through tough times, they still helped a brother out. There is no jealousy between us."

"Is that where the sharing of women came from?" asked Jasmine.

"It was just a natural progression," said Jackson. "I just wanted the best for them and to see them happy. Before, it was just a thrill; now, we want something more permanent. Someone we can all love."

Jasmine looked at the sincerity in Jackson's eyes and demeanor. It was what she was looking for, too, but she didn't know how it would work out for her. She saw what her friend Kiera had with the guys but didn't know if that kind of relationship would work for her.

After clearing the table and washing the dishes, Jackson and Jasmine sat on the couch overlooking the pool through the sliding glass doors. The sun displayed hues of purple and red across the sky.

"I want to apologize for getting upset before, but know that I really care for you. We all do. Enough about me. Tell me what's going on with you and your fiancé."

Jackson held Jasmine's hand while she spoke.

"I met Todd as I was building my business. He brought in a client, and we hit it off. He would tell me everything, but something has changed. He's been keeping secrets from me. I think there's a wall that's blocking our relationship from going deeper." Jasmine looked down. "I want it to work with Todd and me, but I think there's something missing. That's why we decided to do the free week thing where we are free to do whatever we want to do. We can explore sexually and physically with anyone."

Jackson looked at Jasmine with a puzzled look on his face. "What the hell is a free week Jasmine?"

"I know it's hard to understand Jackson, but this is just something that I needed to do."

"So, let me get this right. You can fuck anyone you want this week, and next week, you go back with him."

"Well, yeah now that you put it that way."

"I'm going to be real with you, Jasmine. We like you and have for a while. The sexual chemistry is off the chain; I've personally been trying to fuck you since college," said Jackson. It made Jasmine smile that he wanted her.

"I didn't know it was like that; I just thought you guys looked at me as a kid sister," Jasmine said.

"Maybe back then," said Jackson, "but now, yo ass is fine, and you are smart as hell. Look at you, starting and running your own business. I just don't want to fuck you, though, I want you to consider us as an option."

"What kind of option?" asked Jasmine.

"A long-term option," said Jackson. Jasmine looked into Jackson's eyes.

"I'll think about it," said Jasmine. With that, Jackson nodded.

Jackson lifted his hands to touch Jasmine's cheek. "You and the guys have been so honest and open. I feel a connection with you all that I haven't felt before." Jackson slid his hand to the neck of Jasmine and slightly pulled her closer to his mouth.

"Jasmine, let me kiss you."

"I was hoping you would," said Jasmine.

Jackson moved in closer, breathing Jasmine in. He could smell the shea butter that she wore. He moved closer because he couldn't stay this near to Jasmine without capturing her mouth. He started gently with the kiss. He wanted to savor the sweet honey taste of her.

Jasmine was shocked at how gentle the football giant was with her mouth. The attraction was so strong that she wanted to grab his damn face and suck his tongue until she got enough but decided to let him lead. She moaned in excitement and anticipation. Jackson took the kiss deeper. A fire ignited inside him, and he started to thrust his tongue and explore without abandonment.

Jackson reluctantly disconnected his mouth from hers.

"Let's finish this in the room," said Jackson as he stood up.

She could see the bulge of his groin through his jeans. She tried to look away but was captivated by the man that stood in front of her. His almond-colored skin glistened in the light of the dawning of the sun. His jeans stretched tight over his toned thighs and calves. *His ass is fine,* thought Jasmine.

Breaking from the stare, she said yes.

Jackson scooped up Jasmine and hurried to his bedroom. He moved fast for a big guy. He couldn't wait another minute to get inside of her, but he wanted to make sure that she had her pleasure first.

Jasmine couldn't wait either; her panties were soaked.

Jackson took Jasmine's shirt off first. He then unsnapped the bra, and her large breasts tumbled from the cups.

"Damn Jasmine, I didn't know you were stacked like that," said Jackson.

Jasmine liked the way Jackson admired her breast. He bent to take one in his mouth then the other.

Between licks, he said, "You are so fine." Jasmine let him sample the goods. Jackson then removed her panties. "You look good everywhere," said Jackson in a low, guttural voice.

"Jackson, please give me that damn cock," said Jasmine. "I've been staring at it all night; it looks like a python in your pants," said Jasmine with a smile.

"Fuck, Jasmine. I don't want to rush. I waited a long time for this," Jackson said as he grabbed her by the pussy. Jackson bent to his knees and looked up at Jasmine, saying, "Ride my face," and he put his face in between her legs. "Your pussy tastes so damn good, just like Mike said it did."

Jasmine began to moan as Jackson thrust his tongue deeper and deeper into Jasmine's cunt. Jasmine put both her legs on Jackson's shoulders. "Damn Jasmine, I can eat this pussy all night."

"Oh, oh!" Jasmine began to shake. Jackson slid a finger into Jasmine.

"Yo pussy is so tight. Jasmine, you don't know what you are doing to me." Jackson kept licking her clit and fingering her pussy. "You gon' cum for me like you came for my brothers?"

"Yes, yes," said Jasmine as she shuddered her release while screaming his name: "Jackson, Jackson, Jackson."

After Jasmine's orgasm weaned, Jackson detached Jasmine's pussy and legs from his face. "Jasmine, get on the bed with your ass in the air," Jackson commanded.

This turned Jasmine on. She flew to the bed and positioned her head down with her ass in the air as high as she could get it while arching her back. She wanted him so badly.

Jackson took off his clothes. He could see Jasmine's pussy juices running down to her ass. He would take care of that real soon. Jasmine could feel Jackson entering the bed. She anticipated his fat cock being inside of her. But when she felt his tongue lick her from clit to ass, she wasn't disappointed either.

"I just had to get another fucking taste of you," said Jackson. He ate her pussy and her booty until Jasmine started whimpering.

"Please Jackson," begged Jasmine, "I need that dick."

"Oh, you do?" asked Jackson, moving closer to Jasmine on the bed. He spread her ass cheeks to see if she was ready for him. Then, he put his cock inch by inch into her tight pussy. There was some resistance, so he played with her clit. Jasmine relaxed to accommodate the python that had entered her pussy. Jasmine could feel Jackson's dick making room. At first, he was still to allow her to stretch. Then he started moving.

"Damn yo pussy is so tight. I'm about to bust already," said Jackson. He grabbed Jasmine's soft ass as he worked her cunt with his dick. He gave her ass a few slaps which made Jasmine reel. "Yes, yes, yes!" shouted Jasmine.

Jackson worked his cock even further into her hilt. His length and girth stretched her cunt wide open.

"My pussy is so open!" screamed Jasmine as she took more and more of that dick.

Jackson pounded Jasmine as he bent to grab her tits. He could tell she was about to shoot off by the way her pussy was tightening on his dick. His groin felt heavy like it was about to blow, so he pistoned inside of Jasmine moving faster and faster. "Give me that pussy!" shouted Jackson.

"Yes, yes," said Jasmine as she pushed back into him. Jasmine's orgasm built and built as Jackson thrust deeper and deeper inside of her.

"Cum for me, Jasmine."

Jasmine shuddered and came so hard she screamed. She didn't know what she screamed, but she did. This triggered Jackson's orgasm. He groaned deep and guttural as he released white-hot pleasure inside of Jasmine. He knew that this was more than just a fucking. This was deeper. He didn't quite understand the feelings Jasmine had stirred in him.

He lifted Jasmine and placed her on his chest.

"You are amazing," he whispered. Jasmine turned her head and kissed his cheek. She had a lot going on with Todd but she would push that to the back of her mind for now. She would focus on this moment with Jackson.

Chapter 11: Altogether in Passion

Jasmine awoke to the soft breathing of Jackson and his large, muscled arm draped around her waist. She enjoyed the feel of him and felt cherished.

Today would be the day that they would rescue Todd and hopefully make some sense of what was going on. However, her focus was not on Todd but on the men who had protected her, provided for her, and satisfied her.

Something inside of Jasmine had changed, but she wasn't sure what. Jasmine gently slid out of the bed as not to wake Jackson. He only moaned a little bit in protest of her leaving but didn't wake.

She looked at the beautiful, protective man once more before going to the bathroom.

Jasmine stood in the shower as the light droplets of water poured over her face. Her mind was scattered. She thought about Todd and the relationship they had for years. She loved him, but his secrets caused a rift in their relationship. Could she trust him with her future and ultimately her life? She also thought about the men. Was this just a sexual affair with them or could it be more? She did know they were honest about being hurt and that they wanted someone to love. But what would that look like? She didn't know if she could make that type of relationship work. She saw her friend Kiera do it, but she also knew that Kiera was patient and kind-hearted.

Thought after thought raced through Jasmine's mind as the water flowed. She was almost finished showering when she heard a knock on the door.

"Jasmine, can we talk?" asked Jackson over the water.

"Yes, one second," said Jasmine as she turned off the faucet, toweled down, and stepped out of the shower. She grabbed her robe before stepping into the room. She lost her composure when she saw the men looking at her.

"Oh, I didn't know it would be all of us talking," said Jasmine. Yes, said Jackson as he led her to the bed. Jasmine didn't know what the men wanted and was a little apprehensive. Jackson looked Jasmine in her eyes.

"Jasmine, my brothers and I were talking and realized that we need you in our lives." Jasmine's face was in shock, she felt breathless.

"We know it's only been a couple of days, said Andre, "but we all feel something deeper."

"It's more than a sexual thing, Jasmine: Our hearts and emotions are tied up in this," said Mike. "We understand you've got Todd," said Jackson, "but we want to prove to you how good we could all be together. Can we prove it?" Jackson asked while he bent to kiss her lips. The kiss was sincere but grew into something more. Mike and Andre watched as the passion they felt for Jasmine consumed Jackson.

Breaking from the kiss, Jackson asked, "Can we all be together, right here, right now?" Jackson spoke what everyone was thinking and feeling.

"Yes," said Jasmine, feeling the electricity of emotions and desire flowing in the air.

Jasmine moved back up on the bed and released her robe. The guy stared at her body. Her nipples harden before their eyes. Not only did they stare at her body but they devoured the sight that was in front of them. The men began removing their clothes.

Jasmine laid naked in front of them, she opened her legs and propped them up. She wanted the guys to see how ready she was for them. Her pussy glistened with her juices. Jackson's breath hitched in his throat seeing Jasmine naked.

"You look so damn good," said Jackson as he continued to take his clothes off. Mike and Andre step near the top of the bed, fully naked. Each taking a breast to caress. Their heads bobbed up and down on the buds of Jasmine's taint nipples. Jackson knelt in front of Jasmine. He had to taste her sweet pussy. He licked each fold then sucked the clit in his mouth. Jasmine moaned at the sheer pleasure that raced through her body. She reveled at the licks and sucks that each man rendered. She felt her orgasm growing.

"Jasmine, do you like what Jackson is doing to your pussy?" asked Andre.

"Yes, yes, yes," said Jasmine breathlessly.

"Open your legs wider for Jackson," said Andre as he looked at Jackson fucking Jasmine with his tongue.

"That's good," said Andre after Jasmine opened her legs wider. He continued sucking her nipples.

Jasmine stroked Mike's and Andre's cock, gliding up and down the hard shafts.

"Damn, said Mike, "this feels so good." He looked on as Jasmine stroked his brother's cock. Seeing how he was enjoying it he said, "Jasmine, open your pretty mouth and suck Andre's cock."

Andre brought his dick closer to Jasmine's face.

"Suck it, baby," Andre said.

Jasmine slid his rigid cock in her mouth. She moaned while sucking.

The way Jackson was eating her pussy was sending her over. Jackson pumped his two large fingers inside as he lavished her clit. She started to shake but she kept stroking Mike's cock and sucking Andre's dick. Her senses were overloading. She hadn't felt anything like this in her life. It exceeded the fantasies that she often had. Jasmine's sounds grew as her orgasms got louder.

"Cum for us, Jasmine," said Mike as he looked at Jasmine with her full lips wrapped around his cock.

She moaned and moaned; then, she popped. She came on Jackson's fingers. He continued to pump her until the orgasm weaned a little.

They turned Jasmine on her side. They were eager to get in her pussy and feel the squeeze of her walls. Jackson laid in front of Jasmine while Mike laid in the back of Jasmine.

Andre stood; he wanted to feel Jasmine's mouth on his shaft. Jackson gently caressed Jasmine's face while moving her hair to the side.

"Jasmine, we want you so fucking bad it hurts," said Jackson. He kissed her tenderly at first but became more enthralled as their passion increased. He then put his hand between them to open her tight pussy. He tried to hold back, but her smell propelled his cock deep inside of her. He began stroking. Jasmine felt Jackson's large cock opening her all the way.

"Yes, yes," she said. Then, she felt Mike opening her ass cheeks and a cold jelly at the entrance of her rosette. She never had anal sex before and started to wiggle.

"Jasmine, you have to relax," Mike said as he pressed the tip of his cock in the virgin opening of Jasmine's ass. "You will feel a little pressure at first, but then, it will feel good."

"We all want you so bad," said Mike as he kissed up and down Jasmine's neck.

Jackson was still while Mike inserted his cock into Jasmine's ass.

"Are you in?" asked Jackson. He wanted to move inside of her wet walls.

"Yes," said Mike as his cock pushed deeper and deeper inside of Jasmine's ass.

Jasmine wanted to scream with the double penetration feeling so good, but Andre stuck his length in her mouth. They all moved in unison.

"She's so fucking tight," said Mike as he started to move a bit faster in Jasmine's ass.

"I know," Jackson said as he increased his tempo, too."

"I won't last," said Andre as Jasmine sucked his cock to the point that she almost gagged.

Andre watched Mike fuck Jasmine from the back and Jackson fucking her from the front. This turned him on more. He pumped faster in her mouth. He could hear Jasmine moaning with his cock in her mouth and shivered at the vibrating sensations.

"I'm about to cum," said Andre as he shot his load down Jasmine's mouth. This speared on the guys.

"Cum for us Jasmine," Jackson said as he pounded her from the front.

Jasmine screamed and screamed. Her pussy, clit, and ass united in a multitude of sensations. She blasted off. It was an out-of-body experience. Her mind blanked as she entered a space where time didn't exist.

She came to when she felt Andre and Jackson shooting off their loads inside of her. This triggered another cataclysmic orgasm in her. Jasmine panted and whimpered as they continued to rock her to the core. Jackson and Mike pulled out of Jasmine. Jackson laid Jasmine on top of him.

"Jasmine, that was more than amazing," said Jackson as he kissed her deeply.

Then, she felt someone opening her legs and pushing into her cunt from the back. She moaned into Jackson's mouth.

Andre pounded Jasmine's wet pussy. He held her waist while she held onto Jackson. She panted and moaned her excitement at what they both were doing to her. Her wall squeezed Andre's hard shaft. They exploded together. Andre's and Jasmine's cum leaked onto Jackson. She liked the fact that the guys couldn't get enough of her, and she felt the same way about them. After another round, she and the men were fully satisfied.

Chapter 12: It's All in the Bag

"Sleepyhead, time to get up," whispered Jackson. Jasmine stirred a little but didn't wake up. He looked at the beautiful woman lying next to him. He also looked at his brothers occupying the large bed. He felt complete.

He wanted to make this thing work with Jasmine and his brothers but didn't know about Todd or how to make it work.

Earlier in the day, Jackson made some calls to some of his JAM CrossFit gym clients who were also on the police force. They were more than willing to help him out after offering them a month of free gym passes. They ran a background check on Todd but didn't find anything. They also checked his business and found out that he was in a lot of debt—to the point that his business was on the brink of closing. He then told them everything that was going on with the masked men and

Todd. They said that they could send a few undercover agents to the exchange. They also wanted Jasmine to wear a wire, but he said no because it would jeopardize her life.

He told his brothers and Jasmine everything after speaking with the police. At first, Jasmine was upset, but then she agreed that getting the police involved was a good idea. Plus, they would be undercover, so the masked men wouldn't know anyway.

Jackson continued to think about ways that he and his brothers could be with Jasmine permanently. He liked the fact that she was smart and understood what it took to build a business. Plus, she was caring and thoughtful. He wondered if they could build a family together. It wouldn't be the conventional family that others had, but it would be a family, nevertheless. He wanted to make it work, and he would.

Jackson, Jasmine, Mike, and Andre arrived at the hotel. It was one of the new hotels in the area. Jasmine was in disguise because she didn't want anyone to know who she was. She had a black shawl draped over her head and sunglasses on. She held Jackson's hand while Mike and Andre walked behind her. She felt safe surrounded by tall, well-built men. However, when she walked into the lobby, several hotel guests started to stare.

"I was trying not to be so distracting," said Jasmine, "but you guys look so good that all eyes are on you."

Mike and Andre looked around the lobby to make sure no one was following them.

"Jasmine, this is a nice hotel, but we still have to be careful not to bring too much attention to ourselves. These people could be anywhere," Jackson noted.

A shiver ran down Jasmine's back at the thought of the masked men and being there.

"You don't think we were followed?" asked Jasmine.

"No," Andre said. "The coast looks clear."

Jasmine led the way to the elevator.

"I'm located on the eighth floor."

Everyone piled inside the elevator.

"Hey guys, can you be the lookout while I kiss our Jasmine?" Mike asked.

"Sure," said Jackson and Andre.

They understood that Mike was trying to calm down Jasmine. They blocked the doors while Mike kissed Jasmine's full lips as he backed Jasmine into the elevator. He took her lips slowly and meticulously. He knew that today there would be a lot going on, but the fire that was inside of him could only be quenched with a kiss. His hands roamed up and down her backside. Jasmine moaned at the sensations.

The bell to the elevator halted the kiss.

"This is our stop," said Jackson as he stepped out of the elevator.

They walked side by side down the hallway.

"This is me," said Jasmine as she stopped in front of room 813.

"I can unlock the door if you give me your key," said Jackson. Jasmine handed Jackson the key.

He swiped it near the door, and the entry light turned green. He went into the large room and looked around. He checked to make sure no one was inside waiting for Jasmine.

"Does anything look out of place," asked Jackson?

"No, everything looks exactly how I left it."

Mike and Andre entered the room behind Jackson and Jasmine.

"Nice room, Jasmine," said Andre.

"Thanks," Jasmine said as she looked around the room for her suitcase. The suitcase was inside the closet. Jasmine walked past the bed to the closet to get her suitcase. She then placed it on the bed. The men gathered around Jasmine as she checked her suitcase. "What could it be?" asked Jasmine as she looked around at the man.

"Did you check the side pockets?" asked Jackson. Jasmine checked the entire suitcase but didn't see anything. She dumped the clothes out on the bed.

"I don't understand what the hell is going on," said Jasmine. "It's just a suitcase."

"Let me check and see if something is deep within the sides of the suitcase," said Jackson.

Jackson smoothed his hands along the lining of the suitcase. He felt a lump.

"There's something here. Give me a knife so I can cut it out." The item was enclosed in a hidden pocket.

Mike got a knife from the kitchen in the room. Jackson cut the suitcase to find a small black bag. He held the bag up for all to see. He poured the contents of the bag on the bed.

"Oh shit, look at all these diamonds," said Jackson.

"Jasmine, did you know anything about these diamonds?" asked Jackson.

"Hell no! I am just finding this shit out like you did," said Jasmine. Her face flushed with red at the questions. "Todd did help me pack my suitcase, so maybe he put them in there."

"That's what the men have been wanting, and they are willing to kill for them," Andre exclaimed.

As if on key, Jasmine's phone rung.

Ring, Ring, Ring! Todd's name lit up the caller ID. Jasmine was hesitant to answer and thought about sending it to voicemail but knew that Todd's life was in danger. Being brave, she answered.

"Who the hell is this and where's Todd?!" screamed Jasmine into the phone.

"Do you have my fucking stuff?" asked the man on the phone.

"I do, but do you have Todd? Is he okay?" asked Jasmine.

"Listen here, you bitch. Get me my stuff, or you and your man will die! Meet me tonight at 7:00 underneath the bridge on 55th Street. Don't bring the police if you want to live." Then, he hung up. Jasmine looked down at the phone. She wanted to scream but knew that she had to be strong for Todd.

"Those bastards want their stuff, or they will hurt Todd," said Jasmine with dismay.

"This is fucked up," said Andre.

"It's okay," said Jackson, "we will exchange the diamonds for Todd and everything will work out. The man on the phone still doesn't know about us."

Mike hugged Jasmine. "We'll get through this together, said Mike as Jasmine leaned closer to him.

Chapter 13: The Exchange

It was 7:25 pm. Jasmine sat in her car. *What the hell am I doing here?* Her fear started to creep in. *Maybe I should have let the police handle this.* Her hands started to sweat as she gripped the steering wheel tighter. The bag of diamonds laid on the seat. Jackson was hiding in the back seat.

"You alright Jasmine? " asked Jackson, seeing her fidgeting with the radio.

"Yes," said Jasmine in a quiet voice, not wanting anyone to hear her and Jackson talking.

"Try not to worry, Jasmine; the police are here. Plus, Andre and Mike are behind us in the car."

"Do you see anyone besides the homeless people that are normally here?"

"Not yet," said Jasmine.

About 10 minutes later, a black SUV pulled up toward Jasmine's car. Two masked men with Glocks got out of the car on each side. There were two people in the back of the SUV that Jasmine couldn't see. The man that came from the driver side swirled his finger around to indicate to Jasmine to roll the window down.

"You must be Jasmine," snarled the masked gunman. "We've been looking for you. Do you have our fucking stuff?"

"You mean the diamonds?" said Jasmine.

"Give me the fucking diamonds!" screamed the masked man. "I am tired of playing games with you!"

"Bring out Todd," said the masked man to the backseat passenger. The man got out of the car dragging a battered and beaten Todd.

"Oh, my God. Todd!" screamed Jasmine. His eyes were swollen. His face was black and blue. Dried blood formed around his mouth. The back passenger held a gun to Todd's head.

"Jasmine, I'm okay," said Todd through clenched teeth. "Just give him the diamonds. I am so sorry to put you in this mess, baby. You deserve better."

"Hey, shut the hell up, Todd. We ain't got time for that shit right now. Jasmine, get out of the car and give us the fucking diamonds."

Jasmine looked around at the men with the guns. She was visibly shaken and mad.

"Hurry the fuck up," said the masked man. Jasmine's hand shook as she reluctantly reached for the door. Jackson whispered from the backseat, "Don't worry, I'm here." Grabbing the bag of diamonds from the seat, Jasmine opened the car door and stood up.

"What a pretty lady," said the masked man as he looked at Jasmine from head to toe. "Too bad she has to die. Shoot her and take the diamonds. Oh, and don't forget to kill Todd. They shouldn't have stolen from me."

Shots rang out everywhere and filled the night sky. Jackson jumped from the backseat of the car to protect Jasmine, but it was too late. Jasmine laid on the ground with blood splattered on her chest.

"Jasmine!" screamed Jackson. *Please be okay. Please be okay.* Tears ran down his cheeks. He didn't get the chance to tell her how much she meant to him, and now, it might be too late. He checked her pulse. It was faint, but she was alive for now. He let out a deep breath, then covered her body with his. He had to keep her safe. He didn't know how bad her injuries were but he would get her to a hospital. Shots continue to be heard. Sirens and lights filled the air. Minutes later, he felt someone lifting him up. He tried to fight back but stopped once he heard the sound of his brother's voice.

"Leave me alone!" he shouted.

"Take care of Jasmine first because she is hurt!"

"It's okay," said Andre. "I got you. Mike is with Jasmine in the ambulance headed to the hospital." Jackson felt like he was in a daze. His head was spinning.

"I didn't protect her, man. That was the one thing that we said we would do." Andre could see the hurt in Jackson's eyes.

"What the fuck? Now, we probably lost her forever." Jackson clenched his fists.

"We're gonna get those fuckers," said Jackson.

"Calm down, brother. The masked men are dead. The police shot them. We have to get to the hospital to check on Jasmine. We have to be there for her."

Coming to his senses, Jackson agreed: "Yeah, let's go."

Chapter 14: At the Hospital

The machines beeped loudly as Jasmine's small body laid in bed. Jackson, Andre, and Mike watched Jasmine extensively. It had been two days since the shooting had taken place. They were questioned separately and gave statements but weren't charged because they had informed the police early on about the diamonds and what was going down.

"Jackson, do you think we'll get a chance to tell Jasmine how we feel about her?" asked Andre. He sat in the chair next to Jasmine's bed with his head in his hand looking down at the tiled floor of the hospital room.

"Brother, we have to be strong," said Jackson as he caressed Jasmine's cheek. A tear slipped from his eye. He felt guilty for not acting quickly enough to prevent Jasmine from being shot. It would be his fault if Jasmine didn't want to stay with them, but he hoped she would one day forgive him.

Mike walked into the room. "I checked with Jasmine's doctor, and he said that she should make a full recovery if she pulls through tonight. The bullet grazed her subclavian artery but with the surgery, it was patched up. Jasmine did lose a lot of blood and had to be given a transfusion.

"Thanks for checking on things, Mike," said Andre as he released the breath that he had been holding. Mike knew that the information would comfort his brothers.

"The thing is guys, Jasmine has to fight. She has to *want* to live," said Mike with a look of

exhaustion creasing his forehead.

"We need to show her that there is a reason to live," said Jackson. He moved toward the guys. "We can do this by being here for her and making sure she has everything she needs."

"It's more though," said Andre. "I love Jasmine and want to spend whatever time it takes to show her. Jackson looked at his brother and saw the love in his eyes for Jasmine.

"I love her, too," said Jackson, finally admitting out loud what he felt in his heart since he saw her at the club.

"Me three," said Mike as he sat the clipboard with Jasmine's paperwork on the table. As Mike continued, he said, "I thought it was just a physical connection with her at first, but deep down, I knew it would be more. She does something to me that no other woman has." Mike stared at Jasmine in the bed.

Jasmine could hear the declarations of love from each man, but sleep held her hostage. Plus, the oxygen mask muted her words. She wanted to break free. Jasmine took all her strength to move. She wiggled her toes a little. Would it be enough?

Mike's eyes roamed over Jasmine's body and landed on her pink painted toe sticking from underneath the cover. He noticed it moved. "Guys! Guys! I think I just saw Jasmine wiggling her toe."

The men rushed to surround Jasmine. "Are you sure?" asked Jackson.

"Yes, I am sure. Let's see if she will do it again."

"Jasmine? Jasmine, we are here for you, baby," said Jackson as he leaned across the bed to look her in the eyes.

"She moved her toe again," said Andre. Mike was on the other side of the bed.

"Let's call the doctor to remove the oxygen mask." A doctor and a nurse came into the room.

"Jasmine moved her toe, and we need to see if she can talk," said Mike.

"Let's examine her first," said Dr. Stephen.

Jackson, Andre, and Mike sat quietly as the doctor and nurse examined Jasmine. The doctor removed the oxygen mask from Jasmine's face, and she started to come to.

"Jasmine, I am Dr. Stephen. Do you know where you are and how you got here?"

Jasmine's voice was quiet. "Nurse Cathy, can you bring a cup of water for Jasmine?"

The nurse brought the water and Jasmine drank it through a red and blue straw.

"Jasmine, do you know how you got here?" Dr. Stephen asked again. Jasmine cleared her throat.

"Yes," she squeaked out. "I was shot." Jasmine looked around at the people in the room.

"May I have a moment with the men?" asked Jasmine.

"Yes, of course," Dr. Stephen said. With that, Dr. Stephen and the nurse left the room.

The men gathered around Jasmine in the hospital bed. Jackson lingered back because he felt guilty for not protecting Jasmine. The room was quiet besides the low beeping of the patient monitors. Jackson moved forward toward Jasmine.

"I'm so sorry for not protecting you." His face was strained with agony. "But Jasmine, I swear on my life that I will protect you and love you forever if you give me and my brothers a chance. I know I don't deserve your forgiveness, but please know that I love you and will do anything for you." Jackson stepped away from the bed to regain his composure.

Andre stepped up. "Jasmine, when I thought that we had lost you, my world shattered. I couldn't think, eat, or do anything. I love you with my whole heart, even though it's only been a short time since we have reconnected." Andre rubbed Jasmine back as he spoke. "We want you to be a part of our lives. We know it will take time to heal and move past everything that has happened, but we will wait for you. Andre released his hand from Jasmine's back and made room for Mike at the bedside.

"Jasmine, a lot has happened in the past few days." Jasmine looked down at her hands. She had a million questions to ask, but right now she needed peace. She didn't want to think about Todd or the men.

"Jasmine, I know it's a lot to think about, but we do love you. You are always on my mind. At first, I tried to deny the feelings I have for you, but when you weren't with us, they slammed into my heart. I can't think of a day without you. I love you, Jasmine, and hope we can build a family unit with my brothers in the future. You make us all so happy," said Mike.

Clearing her throat, Jasmine said, "Guys, thank you for letting me know how you feel, but I need time to process. I don't know what happened to Todd, my fiancé, and now, you are telling me that you all love me. It's a bit much. I just need time."

Jasmine looked around the room at the men. She closed her eyes and let out a breath she had been holding. "Would you please leave, so I can rest?"

"But Jasmine, we need to take care of you," said Jackson.

"No, the nurses and doctors will take care of me just fine. Please leave!"

Without further hesitation, the men left the hospital room.

Chapter 15: Home Sweet Home

It had been a week since Jasmine returned home from the hospital. She woke up in her bed and stretched. She was still a little sore from the gunshot wound, but all in all, she was okay. It felt weird that Todd wasn't there, and the house felt very large, but she was glad to be alive. She hadn't talked to the men in over a week. They had tried to call her, but she sent the calls to voicemail. She didn't know what to do.

During the week, she found out that Todd was in jail for dirty business dealings, and the diamonds were from a robbery where someone was killed. The police didn't think Todd robbed the place but may have been an accomplice in helping to sell the diamonds. He owed a lot of people money and started doing illegal deals. She knew he was keeping secrets but didn't know that the secrets would endanger her life.

She had talked to him on the phone. He would be in jail for two to five years. He asked for her forgiveness, but she told him never to contact her. The pain was too deep to start over with him.

"Jasmine, are you awake?" asked Denise while knocking on the door.

"Yes, come in," said Jasmine as she fixed her robe.

"Denise, thank you for taking care of me. I don't know what I would have done without your help."

"No problem, Sis. You have taken care of me for a long time, so I'm glad I could return the favor." Denise looked at her sister. "How are you feeling today?"

"Much better," said Jasmine as she passed her hand through her hair. "I am still in a little pain, but I am feeling better."

"Jasmine, I know it's none of my business, but it looks like more than the physical pain that you are in. Your heart looks like it is broken. You are sad most of the day, and you haven't been yourself."

"I know, Denise. I am just so confused. I still have feelings for Todd, but after everything, he broke my heart."

Denise sat on the bed next to Jasmine: "I understand, Sis, but what about the men? They love you so much. They have been by to check on you daily. Now, it is a little unconventional, but I think it will work out. How do you feel about them?"

"I don't want to admit this, but I love them all. I feel so guilty because of how I felt for Todd. I don't want to jump into another relationship because of what I just went through."

On one hand, Jasmine loved Todd, and he almost got her killed; on the other hand, the guys had been honest and had protected her with their lives.

"Jasmine, you have time to figure things out," Denise said as she embraced her sister. She wished she could do more to take away the pain. "Today, you need to get some rest. I made breakfast if you feel like eating."

Chapter 16: At the Salon

Things were almost back to normal. Jasmine was at her salon sweeping the back office, but the happiness and joy she felt weren't there. She was missing a big part of something or someone. She hadn't talked to the men, and she missed them.

"Jasmine, what's going on?" asked Imani.

"You are not yourself, and it's all over your face."

"I have a lot on my mind, said Jasmine."

"I understand," said Imani soberly. Jasmine continued sweeping the floor. "Everything will be alright."

Suddenly, there was a commotion in the salon. The catcalls from the women could be heard over the music. Jasmine rushed to the front of the salon to see what was going on. Jackson, Mike, and Andre stood at the front desk looking like Chippendale models.

"Jasmine, these gentlemen were looking for you," said Stephanie with a wink.

"Thank you, Stephanie. I can see them in my office." Jasmine walked down the middle of the salon with the three men towering behind her. The clients all turned to look. Some smiled while others pointed, winked, and waved.

"Behave ladies," said Jasmine as she walked past. Jasmine entered her office and closed the door after everyone was inside.

"Guys, what are you doing here?" asked Jasmine with a pensive look on her face. "I was going to call and check to see how things were going, but the salon got busy." Jasmine tucked her hair behind her ear.

"Jasmine, we still have feelings for you," said Jackson, "and they are not going away. We tried not to bother you and give you time to decide what you want, but there's a pull between us, and it gets stronger every day." Jackson moved toward Jasmine to hold her hand. "I know I should have done more to protect you, but I swear on my life that if you give me the chance, in the future, I will."

Andre gently claimed Jasmine's other hand. "Jasmine, All I know is I love you and want to be with you. This time has further reinforced the feelings that I have. You are business smart and compassionate. Plus, you are caring."

Mike moved in between Jackson and Andre. "Jasmine, you mean the world to me and us. Would you marry us?"

Jasmine's eyes widened and filled with tears. She was speechless. "I . . . I . . . love you and will marry you all!" shouted Jasmine as she flung her arms around all the men at once in a big hug. "I have known for a while, but I was afraid to give you my heart."

Jasmine placed her hand over Jackson's heart. "Jackson, you protected me from stray bullets with your life, and that's one of the reasons why I love you."

She moved in front of Andre and placed her hand on his check. "Andre, you lifted my spirits while I was in the hospital. The nurses told me about how you told me jokes while I was asleep."

Jasmine looked up and at Mike while holding both his hands. "Mike, thank you for taking care of me at the hospital. You looked over my charts and kept watch over my vitals."

Mike grabbed Jasmine for a long desired-filled kiss. Next, Jackson gazed into her brown eyes then took her lips slowly and seductively. Lastly, Andre eagerly kissed her multiple times.

"Jasmine, we are so happy that you decided to take a chance on us! Can we make this official with dinner and something more?" said Andre with a wink.

"Yes," Jasmine said as she gazed at the men that she would have forever.

Epilogue

One year later......

"Jasmine, the wedding was so beautiful!" said Denise. They looked at the people mingling at the reception located at Sky Hall in downtown Atlanta. Kiera and her men stood talking near the casement windows. Drapes ran from the ceiling to the floor in the grand ballroom. Glass chandeliers reflected light, giving the hall a glow. Champagne flowed from tranquil fountains. People swayed from left to right as the band played John Legend's song "All of Me."

"Thank you, Denise," Jasmine said. "I'm so happy everything came together." Jasmine looked to the left at the men she had joined in matrimony.

"Jasmine, you're staring; they're yours now," said Denise with a laugh.

"Yes, I know," said Jasmine as she smoothed the lace on her dress down. "I can't believe how my life has turned out."

Jasmine's life couldn't get much better. Her salon was doing great. She was able to hire a new manager. She also opened another location in Decatur, Georgia. The men's CrossFit gyms were on target to hit $10 million in revenue. They had opened a headquarters in Atlanta where they moved to be with Jasmine. Most importantly, she was with men who loved her and would protect her with their lives. Plus, she trusted the men wholeheartedly.

All sides of the family came to support, even though it was unconventional. Jackson legally married Jasmine, but she took the last name of all the guys.

"Jasmine, I am so happy for you," said Denise.

Jasmine looked up to see Jackson, Mike, and Andre crossing the room to approach their target. "Excuse us," said Jackson, "can we borrow our wife?"

Denise giggled like a schoolgirl and said, "Of course! She's all yours."

Jackson held Jasmine's hand and led her to the dance floor. He stood in front of Jasmine while Mike and Andre stood to the sides. They gently placed their hands on her waist.

"Thank you for loving us, Jasmine," said Jackson.

"Thank you for loving me," said Jasmine.

They would have Jasmine to have and to hold from this day forth. No further words were spoken; they let the words from the song speak for them. *All of me loves all of you.*

Read the next book in the series: "Ours to Love" The Brotherhood Series: Book 3

Link to book: www.amazon.com/dp/B09HQ87Q6C

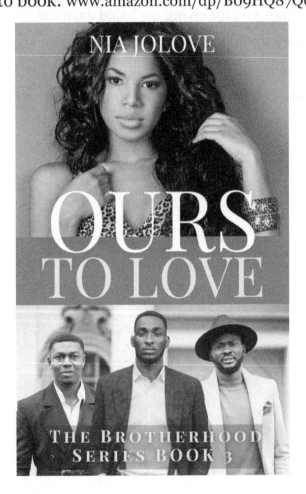

The Diva:

Denise a rising star didn't want three sexy bodyguards watching her every move. She also didn't want the stalker who has been threatening her life. But what she got was an affair with the few the proud that will make her scream.

The Bodyguards:

Zack, Cash, and Blaze former marines turn bodyguards are ready to protect, serve, and share. But not a Diva actress with a chip on her shoulder.

Will Denise lose her life to a stalker or her heart to the brothers.